The King on the Hill
Written and Illustrated by Darren Lewis
Edited by Tanya Bullock

For my lovely wife, Tanya, my amazing children, Katia and Jake and my cool mum, Megan. With love D.L.

The king was feeling glum.

Sitting on a throne all day was
very boring indeed.

...a blanket of snow fell thick and fast.

The snow gave the king
an amazing idea!

He ran as fast as his little legs could carry him.

He took an old shield
from the wall.

He found a bottle of Shield Shine,
on the kitchen shelf.

The king polished his shield until he could see his face in it.

He raced outside, jumped on his shield and down the hillside he went.

Down the hill and through the forest
he flew.

Faster and faster he went, through the village and towards the market place.

Crash, bang, wallop! The king left a right
royal mess behind him.

He zoomed out of the village...

... and across snowy fields.

He slid down one hill...

... and then another.

WOOOOOOOSHHHH!!!!!!

He looped the loop...

...slipping and sliding in all directions.

WOOOOOOOSHHHH!!!!!!

He sped into a cave...

...and along something really spikey.

Whatever could it be?

Oops!

Out of the dragon's cave he whizzed and across a frozen lake.

At last he came to a stop.

Oh no!

Poor old king.

After such a big adventure,
he was glad to see his little
castle again.

The End.

ZZZZZzzzzz

If this book has lived up to your expectations, please would you consider leaving a review? Amazon.com for US or Amazon.co.uk for UK. It really makes all the difference. Thank you!

Hometown Books
ISBN: 978-1999624903

2018

Artwork by Katia and Jake.

The King on the Hill

In
A Kingdom for a Horse

PURPLEY
And the
EEBS

Coming Soon From
Hometown Books